39 Kids on the Block

Roses Are Pink
And You Stink!

Look for these and other books
in the **39 Kids on the Block** series:

39 Kids on the Block

Roses Are Pink And You Stink!

by Jean Marzollo

illustrated by Irene Trivas

SCHOLASTIC INC.

New York Toronto London Auckland Sydney

ISBN 0-590-42725-3

Copyright © 1990 by Jean Marzollo.
All rights reserved. Published by Scholastic Inc.
APPLE PAPERBACKS is a registered trademark of Scholastic Inc.
39 KIDS ON THE BLOCK is a trademark of Scholastic.

12 11 10 9 8 7 6 5 4 3   2 3 4 5/9

Printed in the U.S.A.   40

First Scholastic printing, February 1991

Thirty-nine kids live on Baldwin Street.
They range in age from babies to teenagers.
The main kids in this story are:
Michael Finn,
Donna Finn,
Mary Kate Adams,
Jane Fox,
Fizz Eddie Fox,
Kimberly Brown,
Rusty Morelli,
John Beane,
Maria Lopez,
and Lisa Wu.

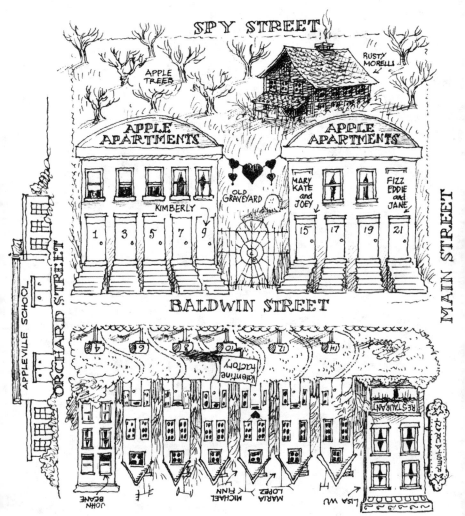

Chapter 1

Michael Finn opened his eyes and put on his glasses. His glow-in-the-dark clock said five o'clock.

"Wake up, Sneaky," said Michael. "It's time to go to work."

Sneaky was a green snake puppet. Michael's dad had won him at the street fair.

"What do you want for breakfast?" Michael asked Sneaky.

Michael put his hand inside Sneaky's head. He gave Sneaky a high voice.

"A toy car," said Sneaky.

"Let's go," said Michael, getting out of bed.

He had to follow two rules when he got up early.

Rule number one: No noise. If he was quiet, he could get up and do things.

Rule number two: No mess. If he was careful, he could fix cold cereal in the kitchen.

Michael tiptoed down the hall past his sister's room. Donna's door was closed. Her room was quiet.

Donna's college banner hung on the door. It said STATE because Donna went to the state university.

Michael was surprised the banner was still there. Donna had been kicked out of college.

She'd been home for a month. During that time she spent a lot of time crying in her room.

Michael didn't know why Donna had had to leave school. His parents wouldn't talk about it. They thought Michael was too young to understand.

That made Michael mad.

At school Michael was the smartest kid in his class. He could read better than anyone else.

And he knew a lot of facts. For example, he knew that real snakes eat mice, not toy cars.

Michael peeked into his parents' room. His father's feet were sticking out of the covers. His mother was snoring.

Last night Michael had heard them yelling at Donna in the living room. Then he had heard Donna run to her room and slam her door. She had started crying again.

Michael wanted to help.

But how could he help if he didn't know what the problem was?

Chapter 2

In the kitchen Michael ate a bowl of puffed rice. Sneaky ate a small fire engine.

Michael looked out the window. It was still dark.

Michael's friend Mary Kate lived across the street. Michael wished her light would go on.

He wished Mary Kate would wave at him. He wished he could invite her over before school. She could work at Michael's valentine factory.

Michael set his bowl in the sink. "Time for work," he told Sneaky.

Michael's desk was the valentine factory. It was covered with paper, glue, glitter, markers, crayons, and a cake pan.

In the middle was a flat, red box. Michael's Christmas bathrobe had come in it.

He opened the box. Inside were three valentines.

Michael and Sneaky had made them. Their plan was to make a valentine for each kid on the block.

There were 39 kids in all, including Michael. So he and Sneaky had to make 38 valentines.

Each valentine was going to have a glitter picture and a message.

The valentine with glitter hearts was for Mary Kate. Michael read it aloud.

Roses are red,
Violets are blue,
You are my friend,
And I like you.

The valentine with glitter ghosts was for Rusty. Rusty lived in the old farmhouse across the street. At Halloween he and his grandmother had had a haunted house party.

> Roses are red,
> Violets are blue,
> The haunted house was great,
> And BOO to you!

The valentine with glitter flowers was for Lisa Wu. It said:

> Roses are red,
> Violets are blue,
> Here are some flowers
> From me to you.

"Thirty-five to go," said Sneaky. "And only two weeks before Valentine's Day. We'd better get busy."

Michael tried to speed up. He cut out a

big white heart. On it he drew a football that said FIZZ EDDIE.

Fizz Eddie was a teenager on the football team. He was named Fizz Eddie because he was good at Phys. Ed.

Phys. Ed. is short for Physical Education, also known as Gym.

Michael outlined the football with glue. Then he sprinkled red glitter on the glue. Next he shook the card into the cake pan.

Some glitter fell into the pan. The rest stuck to the glue. It made the football look sparkly.

Under the football Michael wrote:

> Roses are red,
> Roses are white,
> Let's go, Appleville,
> Fight, team, fight!

Michael also made cards for Maria Lopez, John Beane, and Mary Kate's brother, Joey.

He added the four new cards to the three in the box. That made seven with 31 to go.

"Great job," said Sneaky.

"Thanks," said Michael.

"I bet the kids at school would like to watch you make cards," said Sneaky.

"Really?" asked Michael. "You're sure they wouldn't laugh at me?"

"No way," said Sneaky. "They would want you to teach them how to make cards. They would want to help."

"Maybe you're right," said Michael. "Maybe I could start a valentine factory at school. Mr. Carson would like it because a factory is mathematical. He loves math."

Michael decided to bring the red box to school. He would let his friends peek at the valentines inside. But they couldn't read them. Not until Valentine's Day.

Michael looked at his clock. "There's time to make one more valentine before school," he said.

"Who's it for?" asked Sneaky.

"Donna," said Michael. "To cheer her up." Michael started to cut out another heart.

"Good morning, Mike," said his father, coming into the room.

Michael could smell his father's after-shave. Without looking, he knew his father was already dressed for work.

"Who are you talking to?" asked Mr. Finn.

"No one," said Michael. "I'm making a card for Donna. It says State."

Mr. Finn sighed.

"I know Donna got kicked out of school," said Michael.

His father took a deep breath and let it out. "You should get dressed," he said. "It's almost time to leave."

"Does someone actually *kick* you when you get kicked out of school?" asked Michael.

"Of course not," said his dad.

"Then what *does* happen? And *why* did it happen? I really want to know."

"Michael," said Mr. Finn. "Donna ran into a little trouble. But this is not the time to talk about it. Okay?"

"Why not?" asked Michael.

"Because I said so," said his father.

"Michael, get dressed!" said Michael's mother. She ran into the room and kissed him on the cheek. She was ready for work, too. "I've got to leave. 'Bye! See you tonight!"

Just as she turned to leave, she saw the valentines.

"They're lovely, Michael," she called as she ran out the door.

Chapter 3

Michael Finn and his father stepped outside. The streets were slushy with old snow.

"Today is the first day of February," said Mr. Finn. "Do you know what makes February special?"

"Valentine's Day," said Michael.

"And?"

"And snow," said Michael.

"And?"

Michael loved this game. He and his father called it the "And Game."

"And Lincoln's Birthday," said Michael.

"And?"

The point of the game was to see how many things you could add to the list.

"And Washington's Birthday," said Michael.

"And?"

They were at the bottom of the steps now. Michael saw Mary Kate, Jane, and Fizz Eddie across the street.

He waved to them. He didn't want to play the "And Game" anymore.

"I give up," he said.

Mr. Finn handed Michael the big red box. Michael was already carrying his lunch box.

"Can you carry both of them?" asked his dad.

"I think so," said Michael. He waited to see if his dad would win. The winner of the "And Game" had to say one more thing after the other person gave up.

"And it's Black History Month," said his dad.

Michael grinned. "You win!" he said. Then he called to his friends across the street. "Hey, wait for me!"

Quickly, Michael looked both ways. No cars were coming. So he ran across the street.

"Slow down!" yelled his dad.

But Michael didn't slow down.

Just as he reached the other side, he tripped on the curb.

His glasses went flying. His lunch box went flying. And the big red box went flying, too.

Worst of all, Michael's hands smacked hard against the sidewalk.

"Hey, pal, you okay?" asked Fizz Eddie. Fizz Eddie was Jane's big brother. He walked her and her friends to school every day.

"I think I'm okay," said Michael. "But where are my valentines?" He got up and found his glasses.

"They're up here," said Kimberly. She was a teenager like Fizz Eddie. She had just come out of her building.

Michael looked up. Everything in his lunch box and valentine box had spilled out on Kimberly's steps.

Michael went over to see the damage. It was worse than he'd imagined.

Some of his valentines had landed in slush.

Even worse, his box of juice had broken. Juice had splashed everywhere.

Michael picked up the football valentine. The red glitter was all messed up.

You couldn't even tell it was a football. You couldn't even read the message.

"You okay, Mike?"

Michael looked up through his tears and saw his dad.

"Let's see those hands," said Mr. Finn.

Michael showed his father his hands.

They were all red. They had dirt and ice stuck to them, too. And they hurt.

Fizz Eddie picked up the valentines. He put them in the red box.

"Maybe they'll be okay when they dry," said Kimberly.

But Michael knew they wouldn't be.

"You want to go home?" asked his dad. "Donna's there. She can take care of you."

Michael *did* want to go home. He wanted to forget all about his stupid valentines.

If he went home, he and Sneaky could make something else. Like paper airplanes. Maybe they could have a paper airplane factory.

But Michael shook his head no. "I don't want to miss school," he said. "I have a perfect attendance record."

"Champ, you're tough as steel," said Fizz Eddie. "But let me carry your lunch box, okay?"

"And I'll carry the valentine box," said

Kimberly. "When we get to school, we'll take you to the nurse."

Michael nodded. Every now and then, a sob shook his chest.

He was supposed to be the smartest kid in his class. But he couldn't even run across the street.

His father hugged him good-bye. Michael started off toward school with his friends.

"How come you *made* valentines?" asked Mary Kate. "Don't you know you can buy them? My mom bought me a whole pack of cards."

"And how come you brought them to school today?" asked Jane. "There are two whole weeks before Valentine's Day."

Mary Kate and Jane started to laugh. They didn't mean to hurt his feelings. But Michael was very embarrassed.

He hated to be laughed at.

As soon as he could, he would throw the dumb valentines away.

Chapter 4

Michael sat between Fizz Eddie and Kimberly in the nurse's office. The nurse was helping a kid with a bloody nose. So they had to wait.

Fizz Eddie was whistling. He waved to kids in the hall. He knew everyone.

Maybe he knew about college. Maybe he knew why kids got kicked out of college.

Michael was just about to ask him when the bell rang.

Fizz Eddie and Kimberly got up. "Got

to go," said Fizz Eddie. "Take it easy, champ."

Michael sat alone with his red box and lunch box on his lap.

His lap was too crowded.

Maybe he should throw the red box away. And all the wet valentines inside it.

Michael looked at the nurse's trash basket. It was big enough to hold the box.

He looked inside the box. His valentines had not dried. When they did dry, they'd still be blurry.

Michael sat his lunch box on the chair next to him. Then he tiptoed over to the trash basket. He dropped his box of valentines inside.

The nurse didn't notice.

Michael went back to the chair and sat down.

He looked at the red box in the trash basket. Maybe he should get it back.

Maybe he could fix the valentines.

He didn't know what to do.

All of a sudden the custodian came into the room. He picked up the trash basket and left.

In a few minutes he returned with an empty trash basket.

Tears rolled down Michael's cheeks.

The nurse came over. "Those hands really sting, don't they?" she said.

She thought he was crying about his hands.

Michael nodded. But he was really crying about his valentines.

The nurse washed his hands gently. Then she bandaged them with a pad and long white tape.

Chapter 5

"You look like a boxer," said Mr. Carson.

Mr. Carson was Michael Finn's teacher. He was Mary Kate's, Jane's, and Rusty's teacher, too.

Michael waved his bandaged hands in the air. He liked feeling like a boxer.

Mr. Carson always wore bow ties. Today's tie had little brown animals on it.

"Raise your hand if you know what kind of animals these are," said Mr. Carson.

Everyone gathered round for a close look.

Mary Kate and Rusty raised their hands. So did Michael.

He was feeling much cheerier now. He liked to figure out answers to questions.

Michael raised both bandaged hands and said, "I'm a boxer! Call on me!"

"I'm looking for someone who's quiet," said Mr. Carson. "Mary Kate?"

"Cats?" asked Mary Kate.

"Not quite," said Mr. Carson.

"I'm a boxer!" said Michael. "Call on me!"

"Rusty?" said Mr. Carson.

"Dogs," said Rusty.

"Not quite," said Mr. Carson.

"Me! Me!" yelled Michael.

"I don't call on people who shout out," said Mr. Carson.

Michael closed his mouth.

"Michael?" said Mr. Carson.

"Groundhogs," said Michael.

"Right," said Mr. Carson.

Michael smiled. He loved being the smartest kid in class.

"Today is February first," said Mr. Carson. "And tomorrow is Groundhog Day. Who wants to do the February calendar?"

Michael jumped up into the air and yelled, "I DO! I DO! I DO!"

Mr. Carson gave the eraser and chalk to Lisa Wu.

Michael watched her go to the front of the room.

The calendar lines were drawn in white paint on the board. The words and numbers of January were written in chalk. As Lisa erased, only the chalk marks disappeared.

Meanwhile, Lisa and everyone else sang a song to the tune of "Good-night, Ladies." The song went like this:

> Good-bye, January,
> Good-bye, January,
> Good-bye, January,
> See you in a year.

Michael started thinking about time. How long was a year? And what exactly *was* a year?

You couldn't touch it like a glitter valentine.

You couldn't smell it like his dad's aftershave.

You even couldn't see it like the big painting above the chalkboard. Rusty and his grandmother had given the painting to Mr. Carson for Christmas.

A year was a long, long time. Michael wondered if Donna would cry in her room for a whole year.

Lisa walked back to her seat.

Michael looked at the chalkboard. He was surprised to see that the calendar was done. While he was thinking about time, he had stopped paying attention to Lisa.

Lisa had very neat printing. On the calendar she had written *Groundhog Day, Chinese New Year, Lincoln's Birthday, Valentine's Day,* and *Washington's Birthday.*

And now Mr. Carson was saying, "Does anyone know what is celebrated during the whole month of February?"

"I do!" said Michael. "Call on me!"

No other hands were raised. Mr. Carson sighed and called on Michael.

"February is Black History Month," said Michael.

Mr. Carson asked him to write that on the calendar.

But Michael didn't want to do that. His printing wasn't as neat as Lisa's.

"I can't write today," he said, holding up his bandaged hand. "Could Lisa write it for me?"

And so she did.

Michael smiled to himself. He was glad he was smart enough to get Lisa to write for him.

Mr. Carson asked everyone to brainstorm a list of famous black Americans. Brainstorming was like playing the "And Game."

Martin Luther King
Bill Cosby
Whitney Houston
Jesse Ja[...]
Michael
Jack[...]

Mr. Carson liked lists because they were mathematical. When he made lists, he always numbered them.

The list of Famous Black Americans soon looked like this:

1. Martin Luther King, Jr. — civil rights leader
2. Bill Cosby — comedian
3. Whitney Houston — singer
4. Jesse Jackson — politician
5. Michael Jackson — singer
6. Darryl Strawberry — baseball player
7. Florence Griffith Joyner — track star
8. Jackie Joyner-Kersee — track star
9. George Washington Carver — scientist

"We need one more to make ten," said Mr. Carson.

Everyone thought hard.

Suddenly Michael jumped up and

shouted, "Me! I'm black, and I'm the smartest kid in the class!"

"You're too young," said Rusty.

"And you're not famous," said Jane.

"So stop showing off," said Mary Kate.

Everyone started laughing.

Michael hated to be laughed at. He felt stupid and embarrassed again.

How could anyone be so smart and so stupid at the same time?

Why did he do things that made people laugh at him?

He'd never be a famous American. When he went to college, he'd probably get kicked out, too. Just like Donna.

Mr. Carson tapped Michael's back. "Is everyone listening?" he asked.

Michael jumped. He hadn't been listening at all.

Mr. Carson was talking about the valentine box. "I asked who would like to make it," he said.

"Me!" shouted Michael. "I already have glitter and glue! I even have a valentine factory!"

Kids looked at Michael as if he were weird. Some were laughing at him again.

Mr. Carson frowned. "Michael, how many times do I have to say it? I don't call on people who call out."

Michael closed his mouth and got mad at himself again.

Why did his thoughts burst out of him? Why couldn't he hold them back?

Now he'd never get to make the valentine box.

Mary Kate and Rusty had their hands quietly in the air.

Mr. Carson pointed to them. "Mary Kate and Rusty can make the valentine box together," he said.

It's not fair, thought Michael. Mary Kate and Rusty knew how much Michael liked valentines.

They saw him fall down on the way to school. And they saw his glitter valentines. They'd probably copy Michael's idea and make a glitter valentine box.

Chapter 6

When Michael got home after school, his baby-sitter wasn't waiting for him. She was on vacation now that Donna was home.

Michael tiptoed past Donna's closed door. He heard her radio playing quietly.

He was glad he didn't hear any crying.

Michael told Sneaky what had happened at school. Sneaky was very angry.

"Mary Kate and Rusty should have told Mr. Carson to let *you* make the valentine box," he said.

"I know," said Michael. "But what can I do?"

"Let's make mean valentines to put in their ugly valentine box," said Sneaky. "Let's start a Mean Valentine Factory."

"Yes," said Michael. His head immediately filled with mean ideas.

But before he could do anything, he had to take off his bandages. He unwound the tape and looked at his hands. They were much better.

They could make mean valentines. No problem.

Michael cut out a big red heart. On it he wrote,

> Roses are red,
> Violets are blue,
> You look like
> A bottle of glue.

THAT would be for Mary Kate. And it wouldn't have any glitter on it, either.

Then he cut out a big pink heart. On it he wrote:

Roses are red,
Roses are pink,
Rusty Morelli
You stink.

For a second, Michael felt bad. After all, Rusty was his friend. And so was Mary Kate. Maybe he shouldn't make them mean valentines.

But Sneaky said, "Oh, yes, you should. You should make one for everyone in the class instead of everyone on the block."

Michael and Sneaky worked very hard all afternoon. They made fifteen mean valentines.

"Where are you going to store them?" asked Sneaky.

Michael thought fondly of his big red

bathrobe box. He wished he hadn't thrown it away.

He wondered where it was. Had it been taken to the dump? Or burned?

"Forget it," said Sneaky. "For mean valentines you need an ugly box."

Michael looked around the room. He didn't have any empty boxes.

"Maybe Donna has one," said Sneaky.

Chapter 7

Michael and Sneaky went down the hall to Donna's room. The radio was still on.

Michael knocked on the door.

No answer.

He turned the doorknob. The door opened.

Inside, Donna was asleep on her bed.

Michael went over and stared at her.

She looked sad when she was sleeping.

He bent down close. All of a sudden, his sister opened her eyes.

"Michael!" she cried. "What are you doing here? You scared me!"

"I . . . I . . . I . . ." Michael could hardly talk. He had scared himself.

"I was looking for an empty box," he said.

Donna sat up. She was all dressed up.

"Did you go somewhere?" asked Michael.

"I went to a job interview," she said. "Mom and Dad say I have to get a job."

"What kind?" asked Michael.

"Any kind," said Donna.

"Did anybody kick you?" asked Michael.

"Kick me? Why would anybody do that?" asked Donna. She got up and went over to her closet.

There she found an empty shoe box. "Is this okay?" she asked.

Michael looked at Sneaky. Sneaky nodded and said, "That's fine."

"Let me see that cute little snake," said Donna. She put her hand inside Sneaky. She made Sneaky talk in a funny, growly way.

"Hi, Mike," said Sneaky. "What are you going to do with that box?"

"Put some valentines I'm making in it," said Michael.

"Valentines?" said Donna. "How sweet. Can I see them?"

"I don't think you'll like them," said Michael. "They're not your type."

Donna stuck her lip out. "Please?" she said.

"Okay," said Michael.

Donna, Michael, and Sneaky went down the hall to Michael's room.

One by one, Donna read the mean valentines. Some of them made her laugh.

But the more she read, the more worried she looked.

"Why are you making these?" she finally asked Michael.

Michael told Donna the whole story. He told her about his plan to make glitter valentines for all the kids on the block.

He told her about falling down.

He told her he got in trouble in class for speaking out.

He told her he hadn't been picked to make the class valentine box.

At the end his sister said, "And I thought I had trouble."

"What *is* your trouble?" asked Michael.

"I flunked out of college," said Donna.

"What does 'flunked' mean?" asked Michael.

"I failed," said Donna. "I was having too much fun to study. Then exams came and I did badly on all of them. So the college kicked me out."

"Did they actually kick you?"

Donna laughed. She put her arms around her brother and hugged him. "No, that's just an expression," she said.

Michael hated to be laughed at, but he liked to be hugged. So he smiled.

"Did you like college?" he asked.

"I loved it," said Donna. As she spoke, she started to cry. "And now I can't go back. Mom and Dad say I have to get a job. They say I wasted their money and have to pay them back. They say maybe next year I can go back to school and try again."

Seeing his sister cry made Michael want to cheer her up.

"You want me to make a mean valentine for your college?" he asked. He already had an idea for what to say.

"I guess so," said Donna.

"Watch," said Michael. He cut out a big white heart. Blue and white were State's colors. So he picked up a blue crayon and wrote:

Donna Finn,
She is great.
Who do we hate?
We hate State!

Donna laughed, but only a little. Then she said, "Unfortunately it's not so simple. Hate is not the answer. You can't solve your problems by hating your friends. And I can't solve mine by hating State."

Michael frowned. He wanted to hate his friends. But Donna was saying that hating wasn't smart.

Maybe he should be nice to his friends.

Donna must have read his mind.

"I'll tell you what," she said. "You invite your friends over tomorrow after school. You and your friends can make silly valentines for each other. I'll help you."

Michael felt as if he had just been given a gift.

The least he could do now was think of a way to help Donna.

But he couldn't think of anything.

"How can I help you?" he finally asked.

Donna shrugged. "You can't," she said. "I have to figure out what I want to do with my life. Only I can do that."

That night Michael called Rusty, Mary Kate, Jane, Maria, John, and Lisa.

They were the kids in his class who lived on his block.

Michael invited them to come to his house the next day for a party. He said they could make silly valentines at the party.

Everyone wanted to come. Donna talked to the parents. She said she would meet the boys and girls at the school and walk them home.

The next morning Michael woke up at four-thirty. He and Sneaky set up the factory very carefully.

John and Rusty would cut out the hearts.

Mary Kate and Jane would outline them in glue.

Maria and Lisa would add the glitter.

And Michael would write a silly valentine on each one.

It was a perfect plan.

Chapter 8

After school, Michael, Rusty, Mary Kate, Jane, Maria, John, and Lisa rushed outside. They found Donna waiting by the flagpole.

She was talking with Fizz Eddie and Kimberly. They were asking her about college.

"It's cool," she was saying. "But it's hard. When I go back, I'm going to study."

"Hey, champ," said Fizz Eddie to Michael. "Gimme five."

Michael put out his hand and then pulled it back.

"Sorry, champ," said Fizz Eddie. "I forgot about that nasty fall. Are your hands okay now?"

"He's fine," said Donna. "He's going to have a silly valentine party today. Want to come?"

"I'd like to," said Fizz Eddie. "But I've got basketball practice."

"Me, too," said Kimberly. "Catch you later."

Michael wasn't sure if they really wanted to come or not. But he didn't care. Rusty, Mary Kate, Jane, Maria, John, and Lisa wanted to come.

Rusty brought his markers.

Mary Kate brought a fresh box of crayons.

Maria had paper doilies that looked like lace.

John had puffy valentine stickers.

There was just one problem.

"We don't really need those things,"

said Michael. "I've got everything all set up."

"What do you mean?" asked Mary Kate.

"You'll see," said Michael.

But when they got to his house, his friends stayed in the kitchen.

They didn't go to his room to see the silly valentine factory.

"Who's hungry?" asked Donna. She made peanut butter and jelly sandwiches. The kids sat around the counter and ate them.

As they ate, they asked Donna questions.

They asked her about college.

She told them she went to State.

They asked her where she got her earrings.

She said she bought them in her college town.

They asked her how old she was.

She said 19.

They asked her if she had a boyfriend.

She said sort of.

Michael was getting impatient. "Come on, everybody," he said. "Remember the valentines? We have a lot of work to do!"

"Are you engaged?" Mary Kate asked Donna.

"No," said Donna. "But my boyfriend writes to me every day."

Michael didn't know that. And right now he really didn't care. "We have to get started," he said.

"What's your boyfriend's name?" asked Maria.

"Gilliam," said Donna.

"Come on, everybody! Let's go to my room!" shouted Michael.

"Stop yelling at us!" cried Mary Kate.

"We'll come when we want to!" said Lisa.

Michael was so mad he almost blew up. But instead he said, "Please, everybody. Come with me."

Rusty, John, and Mary Kate followed

him to his bedroom. They began to make valentines on Michael's bed.

That wasn't where the valentine factory was. But Michael sat on the bed anyway. He wasn't sure what to do.

Sneaky was lying next to him. Michael didn't touch him.

He didn't know if the others would like Sneaky or not. He was very confused. Things weren't going the way he had planned.

"All right, look," he finally said. "Everyone has a job. John will cut out hearts. Rusty will put glue around the edges. Mary Kate can do the glitter. And I'll write the silly poems."

"I already wrote one," said John Beane. "Listen."

Frogs are green
You are a scream!

"Green-n-n and scream-m-m don't exactly rhyme," said Michael. "But don't worry. I'll write the poems myself."

"I wrote a poem, too," said Rusty. "Listen to mine."

There's a bat
On a hat
On my cat.
Happy valentine,
To a big fat rat!

Michael took a deep breath. "That doesn't make sense," he said. "But don't worry about it. You'll be doing the glue part. John, start cutting out some hearts."

"I don't want to cut out hearts," said John.

"And I don't want to just do the glue part," said Rusty.

"Can't we do what we want?" asked Mary Kate.

"NO!" yelled Michael. He picked up

Sneaky and shook him. "We planned this!" he shouted.

"Stop yelling!" said Rusty.

Michael threw Sneaky at Rusty.

Rusty caught him in the air. He put his hand in Sneaky and made a hissing sound at Michael.

"Snakes don't hiss!" shouted Michael. "Don't you know anything?"

Suddenly Donna and the other kids appeared at the door. "What's going on in here?" asked Maria.

"Nothing!" said Michael. "That's the trouble!" He tried to grab his snake from Rusty, but Rusty wouldn't let go.

"He wants us to do everything his way," yelled John.

"These people are so stupid they can't do anything right!" cried Michael.

"Whoa," said Donna. "That's enough, Michael. Let Rusty have your snake. You come with me into the kitchen. The rest of you, make valentines however you want. We'll be back in a few minutes."

Chapter 9

Michael threw himself down on the couch.
He buried his head in a pillow.

But he didn't cry. He was too mad to
cry. He bit the pillow instead. It tasted dry
and awful.

Donna sat down on the couch next to
Michael.

For a long time, no one said anything.
Then Donna said a very strange thing.

She said, "Thank you very much."

"For what?" Michael said into the pillow.

"For helping me with my problems," said Donna.

"What are you talking about? I didn't help you. I messed up everything."

"You helped me figure out what I want to do with my life," said Donna.

"I did?" Michael sat up and looked at his sister. Was she putting him on?

"You did," said Donna.

Michael could see his sister was serious.

"How did I help you?" asked Michael.

"By having a fit in front of your friends," said Donna.

"That helped you?"

Donna nodded. "When you got so upset, I realized that I knew how to help you," she said. "I even know what to say to you now."

"What?"

"People are smart in different ways.

The way you're smart is in reading and knowing things. That's called book smart."

"I'm the smartest kid in my class," said Michael. He sat up straighter.

"*Book* smartest," said Donna. "But one way you're not so smart is in thinking about other people. You're not people smart. You think your friends are like puppets. Like Sneaky. And that's not smart at all. You have to realize that you can't make other people do what you want them to do."

Michael thought about that. It would be cool if all his friends were like Sneaky.

If his friends were puppets, they would say what he made them say. And they would do what he made them do.

On the other hand, it might be kind of boring.

Michael sighed. Maybe Donna was right.

Donna put her face close to Michael's. "Did you plan this?" she said.

"Plan what?" he asked.

"You, Mom, and Dad planned this to make me think about becoming a teacher," she said.

Michael couldn't believe it. What a crazy idea.

But Donna was serious. Or was she? Actually she was starting to smile.

Suddenly he understood. She was giving him a way out.

"Well . . ." he said.

Of course, he hadn't planned it. And Donna knew that, too. They both knew he had been rotten to his friends.

"Yup," said Michael. He grinned. "Mom and I planned it this morning."

"And now you're going to go back into your room to make silly valentines?"

"Sure," said Michael.

"Without fighting?"

"Sure," said Michael. "That was all part of our plan." And that's just what happened.

Michael and his friends made silly valentines for everyone in class.

Some of the valentines had glitter and some didn't. Some were big and some weren't. Some were drawn in crayon and some were drawn in markers.

They were all different except for two things.

They were all funny. You could tell because everyone was giggling while they worked.

And they were all secret.

They wouldn't be read until Valentine's Day.

Chapter 10

Michael woke up at four forty-five and looked out the window.

Baldwin Street was dark. You couldn't tell it was Valentine's Day at all.

He tiptoed to the kitchen and put three valentines on the counter. One was for his dad, one was for his mom, and one was for Donna.

"What about me?" asked Sneaky.

Michael gave Sneaky a big kiss. "Happy Valentine's Day," he said.

"You, too," said Sneaky. He kissed Michael back.

"Happy Valentine's Day, Sneaky and Mike," said Donna.

She came into the kitchen in her bathrobe. As she sat down on her stool, she saw her valentine. "For me?" she said.

Donna opened her card and read aloud.

Happy valentine to Donna,
Happy valentine to sis,
We'd like to give you
A great big kiss.
From Michael and Sneaky

"Go ahead, boys," said Donna.

Michael and Sneaky kissed her two cheeks.

Donna pulled a small present out of her bathrobe pocket. It was wrapped in valentine wrapping paper. She gave it to Michael.

He unwrapped it and found a new pencil box. Inside were red pencils, red crayons, and a red felt-tip marker. "For being my valentine," said Donna. "And for helping me solve my problem."

Michael felt very proud of himself. He really had helped his older sister. That felt good.

Today was the third day of Donna's new job. She was working as a teacher's aide at a nursery school.

And she loved it.

Kimberly came out of her building with a donut for Fizz Eddie. It had pink frosting on it.

"For you," she said.

Fizz Eddie's cheeks turned as pink as the frosting. He gave Michael, Jane, and Mary Kate a piece and ate the rest himself.

Then he and Kimberly walked ahead. They didn't hold hands.

"Are they going together?" asked Mary Kate.

"I don't know," said Jane. "She calls him every night. But he never calls her. What do you think, Michael?"

Smart as he was, Michael hadn't a clue. So he shrugged and said, "Anything's possible."

The boys and girls from the valentine factory passed out their silly valentines in class.

There was one for every kid in the class. And Mr. Carson, too.

The kids took turns reading valentines. Michael read one to Lisa.

You're my cat,
You're my poodle,
You're my rooster,
You're my noodle.

Lisa read one to Mary Kate.

Where's the queen?
The one who's great?
Here she comes.
It's Mary Kate!

Mary Kate read one to Jane.

Bumble bee,
Please be mine.
Don't sting me,
And we'll be fine!

Jane read one to John.

Strawberry shortcake,
Huckleberry pie,
Peanut butter valentines,
In the sky.

John read one to Rusty.

Two plus one
That makes three,
You're the tomato
In a B.L.T.

Rusty read one to Maria.

Roses are orange,
The sky is green.
Let's take a ride
In a submarine.

And Maria read to Michael.

Happy Valentine
To a boy with a heart
Who sort of got off
To a very bad start.
(But then he fixed it.)

Everyone laughed. For a moment Michael had that old angry feeling. He hated to be laughed at. But then he laughed, too.

After all, it was a silly valentine.

He stood up and read to Mr. Carson.

> Little red hearts
> On your bow.
> You belong
> On a TV show.

Michael felt his valentine was the best of all. But he didn't say that.

Because that would be people dumb. And now Michael was people smart. He could laugh at himself, and he could stop himself from bragging.

Chapter 11

"Today is March first," said Mr. Carson. He had a new bow tie with yellow flowers on it.

"What kind of flowers are they?" he asked.

Kids raised their hands. But not Michael. Not yet.

"Daffodils," said Mary Kate.

"No," said Mr. Carson. "But that's a good guess."

"Forsythia," said Lisa.

"No," said Mr. Carson. "But that's a good guess, too."

Michael raised his hand. Quietly.

"Michael?" asked Mr. Carson.

"Crocuses," said Michael.

"Yes," said Mr. Carson. "Who would like to do the March calendar?"

Michael Finn raised his hand. Again quietly.

All the other kids raised their hands, too. Mr. Carson gave the eraser to Michael.

He went up to the calendar and erased the word February.

Then he erased *Groundhog Day*, *Chinese New Year*, *Lincoln's Birthday*, *Valentine's Day*, *Presidents' Day*, and *Washington's Birthday*.

And everybody sang the calendar song.

> Good-bye, February,
> Good-bye, February,
> Good-bye, February,
> See you in a year.

Michael erased *February is Black History Month.*

Michael felt a little sad that February was gone. He wondered where it went.

Where does time go? He started to wonder.

Does time get stored in boxes?

Is there a big red box marked *February* somewhere?

Is everything that happened in February inside the box?

Does the box get thrown away when February is over?

No, Michael decided. In his mind there was a little red February storage box. He kept his memories in it. He would remember this February for a long time.

But what would happen next February?

He would be a year older.

So would all of his friends.

So would Donna and his parents.

Would he have another valentine factory party?

He was pretty sure he would. And at the party he would let everyone make valentines the way they wanted.

Would he be making things with Sneaky? Maybe. Maybe not.

Maybe he wouldn't play with Sneaky so much next year. Maybe he would be too old for Sneaky.

Would Donna be back at State college? Absolutely. Michael knew that someday his sister would be as good a teacher as Mr. Carson.

Michael imagined a day in the future. Kids were making a list of famous black Americans. On their list was Donna Finn.

And maybe, just maybe . . .

Maybe Michael Finn was on the list, too.

Maybe he was a famous comedian like

Bill Cosby. Or a famous scientist like George Washington Carver.

It was fun to think about all the possibilities.

"What are you thinking about, Michael?" asked Mary Kate.

"Huh?" said Michael.

"Aren't you going to write St. Patrick's Day on the calendar?"

"Oh, sure," said Michael.

Michael wrote as neatly as he could on the square for March 17.

St. Patrick's Day.

His printing wasn't great, but it was good enough.

While he wrote he started wondering about March.

He looked at all the empty squares in the calendar.

Would they be filled with good things or bad things?

Time would tell.

Maybe time was like a puppet.

Maybe you could put your hand in time and make good things happen. For example, you could invite kids over to your house.

Maybe you could give time your own special voice.

You could say, "What do you want to play?" instead of "Do it my way."

You could even say, "I have a dream," like Martin Luther King, Jr.

As Michael went back to his desk, he smiled to himself.

He had a wonderful feeling that anything was possible.

More fun with
39 Kids on the Block
Look for #4!

The Best Friends Club

Maria wants to ask Mary Kate to
come over on Thursday. "Mary
Kate?"
Sharon giggles. "Do you mean
Mountain Dew?" she asks.
    Maria looks at Mary Kate. "What
is Sharon talking about?"
    Mary Kate giggles. "Do you mean
Shasta?"
    Maria wants to cry. She wants to
be Mary Kate's best friend, but Mary
Kate is in the Best Friends Soda Can
Club with Sharon. And Maria can't be
in it!

Here are some other books about the
39 Kids on the Block.

#1 *The Green Ghost of Appleville*

Poor Rusty Morelli.
He just moved into a haunted house.
Should Mary Kate help him?
Or should she just stay away?

#2 *The Best Present Ever*

Mary Kate, Jane, Rusty, and Michael
all want to get the best
present ever! So who will be the
luckiest kid on the block?

#4 *The Best Friends Club*

Sharon is such a show-off!
Why does Mary Kate always want
to be with her? Mary Kate is supposed
to be Maria's best friend!

#5 *Chicken Pox Strikes Again*

A famous author is coming to
the Orchard Street School.
But everyone is getting the
chicken pox!

About the Author

"I like writing about children and their families," says author Jean Marzollo. "Children are never boring. Whenever I get stuck for an idea, I visit a classroom and talk to the kids. They give me millions of ideas, and all I have to do is choose the right one.

"I also like writing about schools and neighborhoods, which are like great big families. People who go to school together and live together learn a lot from each other. They learn to respect each other's differences. Some of my best friends today are people I grew up and went to school with.

"I remember everything about elementary school—my teachers' names, the lamp with painted roses on it that we gave the teacher when she got married, who cried on the playground and why, and how to make fish with finger paint.

"When I write the stories for **39 Kids on the Block**, I draw on my childhood memories and my experiences in schools today. I also live with my two teenage sons and my husband in Cold Spring, New York, a community with strong values and lots of stories."

Jean Marzollo has written many picture books, easy-to-read books, and novels for children. She has also written books about children for parents and teachers and articles in *Parents Magazine*.

About the Illustrator

"Jean Marzollo and I have been the best of friends for more than twenty years, and we have also worked together on many books," says illustrator Irene Trivas. "She writes about kids; I draw them.

"Once upon a time we both lived in New York and learned all about living in the city. Then we moved away. I went off to Vermont and had to learn how to live in the country. But the kids we met were the same everywhere: complicated, funny, silly, serious, and more imaginative than any grown-up can ever be."

Irene Trivas has illustrated a number of picture books and easy-to-read books for children. She has also written and illustrated her own book, *Emma's Christmas: An Old Song* (Orchard).

LITTLE APPLE

BABY-SITTERS

Little Sister™

by Ann M. Martin, author of *The Baby-sitters Club* ®

☐ MQ44300-3	#1	Karen's Witch	$2.75
☐ MQ44259-7	#2	Karen's Roller Skates	$2.75
☐ MQ44299-6	#3	Karen's Worst Day	$2.75
☐ MQ44264-3	#4	Karen's Kittycat Club	$2.75
☐ MQ44258-9	#5	Karen's School Picture	$2.75
☐ MQ44298-8	#6	Karen's Little Sister	$2.75
☐ MQ44257-0	#7	Karen's Birthday	$2.75
☐ MQ42670-2	#8	Karen's Haircut	$2.75
☐ MQ43652-X	#9	Karen's Sleepover	$2.75
☐ MQ43651-1	#10	Karen's Grandmothers	$2.75
☐ MQ43650-3	#11	Karen's Prize	$2.75
☐ MQ43649-X	#12	Karen's Ghost	$2.75
☐ MQ43648-1	#13	Karen's Surprise	$2.75
☐ MQ43646-5	#14	Karen's New Year	$2.75
☐ MQ43645-7	#15	Karen's In Love	$2.75
☐ MQ43644-9	#16	Karen's Goldfish	$2.75
☐ MQ43643-0	#17	Karen's Brothers	$2.75
☐ MQ43642-2	#18	Karen's Home-Run	$2.75
☐ MQ43641-4	#19	Karen's Good-Bye	$2.75
☐ MQ44823-4	#20	Karen's Carnival	$2.75
☐ MQ44824-2	#21	Karen's New Teacher	$2.75
☐ MQ44833-1	#22	Karen's Little Witch	$2.75
☐ MQ44832-3	#23	Karen's Doll	$2.75
☐ MQ44859-5	#24	Karen's School Trip	$2.75
☐ MQ44831-5	#25	Karen's Pen Pal	$2.75
☐ MQ44830-7	#26	Karen's Ducklings	$2.75
☐ MQ44829-3	#27	Karen's Big Joke	$2.75
☐ MQ44828-5	#28	Karen's Tea Party	$2.75
☐ MQ44825-0	#29	Karen's Cartwheel	$2.75
☐ MQ43647-3		Karen's Wish Super Special #1	$2.95
☐ MQ44834-X		Karen's Plane Trip Super Special #2	$2.95
☐ MQ44827-7		Karen's Mystery Super Special #3	$2.95

Available wherever you buy books, or use this order form.

Scholastic Inc., P.O. Box 7502, 2931 E. McCarty Street, Jefferson City, MO 65102

Please send me the books I have checked above. I am enclosing $_____
(please add $2.00 to cover shipping and handling). Send check or money order - no cash
or C.O.Ds please.

Name_____

Address_____

City_____ State/Zip_____

Please allow four to six weeks for delivery. Offer good in U.S.A. only. Sorry, mail orders are not
available to residents to Canada. Prices subject to change.

BLS991